Goal-ge

GRAFFIX

First paperback edition 1999
First published 1999 in hardback by
A & C Black (Publishers) Ltd
35 Bedford Row, London WC1R 4JH

Text copyright © 1999 Michael Hardcastle
Illustrations copyright © 1999 Bob Moulder
Cover illustration copyright © 1999 Mike Adams

ISBN 0-7136-4941-0

A CIP catalogue record for this book is available from
the British Library.

Printed and bound in Spain by G. Z. Printek, Bilbao.

Goal-getter

Michael Hardcastle
Illustrated by Bob Moulder

A & C Black · London

Chapter One

The kick took Eddie's breath away. The pain was so fierce he didn't even cry out.

As the player who'd kicked him melted away towards the wing Eddie collapsed. His coach was slow to reach him and by then Eddie's face mirrored his agony.

Look, are you coming off or staying on? The ref needs to know.

The pain-killing spray was starting to work but Eddie wasn't sure he was going to be able to walk let alone run.

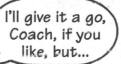

I'll give it a go, Coach, if you like, but...

Jimmy Bolton wasn't listening. He'd already made up his mind to put the sub, Mark, on in Eddie's place. With only ten minutes to go in the League match against Drilby and only one goal ahead he was taking no risks. Eddie limped to the bench, glad to sit down and nurse his injury.

For the next couple of minutes the coach ignored Eddie and just watched the match. Then, without turning to look at him, he suddenly said,

Do you think you've got a low pain barrier? You do claim to suffer an awful lot of knocks. Other players seem to take them in their stride.

Eddie didn't know how to answer that.

They pick on me, just because I'm small. They know I'm good so they want to stop me.

Top footballers have to learn to take care of themselves, to play as if they had eyes in the backs of their heads.

I'll remember that.

Eddie tried not to sound sarcastic. He decided not to ask about the team for Saxilby's next match. The answer might be worse than his injury.

Chapter Two

That evening, Eddie tried to win his mother's sympathy.

I'm having a really bad time with the football team.

You've been kicked haven't you?

How d'you know that?

Eddie knew he'd get no sympathy even if he talked to her all night, so he went in search of his brother. Matthew was practising in the nearby park. For a few moments Eddie watched him trying to chip a football over a rope strung between two trees.

Most times he got the direction wrong and had to retrieve the ball from some distance. Twice in a row, though, the ball neatly cleared the rope. Each time Matthew punched the air with delight. It was as if he'd scored in a real match.

15

Eddie had been about to confide his own problems
to Matthew but realised Matthew wasn't in the
mood to help. As he turned away towards the
house he stumbled over a small stone.
Pain flared in his knee.

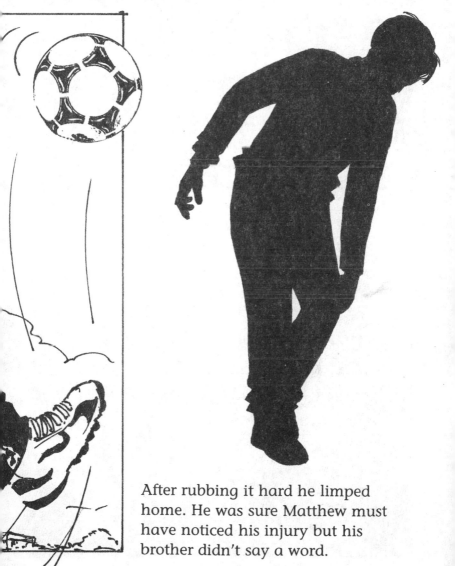

After rubbing it hard he limped
home. He was sure Matthew must
have noticed his injury but his
brother didn't say a word.

It's true. You've just got to sort things out on your own.

But, hard though he tried, he couldn't think of a way to solve his own football problem and it kept him awake half the night.

Chapter Three

To his great surprise, and relief, Eddie was in
the team for the start of Saxilby's vital
away match against Deaton Dynamos.
Jimmy Bolton hadn't even asked
him about his knee injury, but
that was just as well. Eddie still
suffered twinges of pain
when he turned sharply
on the ball. However,
he was sure he could
run off the discomfort
during the match.

Deaton were a very physical side as Eddie soon discovered.

When he received a pass from Danny on the edge of the box he hardly had time to put his foot to the ball before...

...he was clattered to the ground by a tall defender.

Eddie wasn't hurt but he was furious
the ref didn't signal a foul tackle.

When there was a break in play Jimmy Bolton snatched a word with Eddie.

Don't complain to refs. They never listen – they just remember your face and make you pay later.

That remark really annoyed Eddie. It seemed to him that everything and everyone was against him. Even Danny had given him the ball when he was in no position to make good use of it.

I'll show them all – I'll be unstoppable!

He had to wait several minutes before there was an opening and in that time Deaton pounded away at Saxilby's goal. But Elliott, Saxilby's keeper, was in brilliant form and kept everything out.

Then, with most of the Deaton players in Saxilby's half of the pitch, Elliott launched a huge clearance kick to ease the pressure.

The length of Elliott's clearance took most players by surprise; but not Eddie. He judged the bounce well, trapped the ball with his first touch and set off like a sprinter from the blocks.

His pace surprised his opponents. The tall assassin was one of the two players who'd stayed back.

But Eddie easily skipped over his attempt at a scything tackle.

Now he had a clear sight of goal.

The goalie had come off his line to try and save his side.

27

Eddie hardly slowed at all before trying his chip shot. As the ball curved upwards Eddie wished Matthew could have been there to see it. For he knew he'd got it spot on: from the moment the ball left his foot he knew it was a goal.

Eddie leapt high and was still dancing with delight when his team-mates caught up with him. The celebrations would have gone on a long time if the ref hadn't ordered the Saxilby players back to their positions for the restart.

Danny called across to Eddie as they lined up.

Don't forget the coach's big message. If you get one goal, go flat out for the next. You've already got the opposition worried.

Eddie nodded. The coach said that every time and he always tried to follow the advice. He might have succeeded in their very next attack but just as he was stretching for a low cross the ball was diverted by a defender.

Corner!

Roscoe, the Strikers' skipper floated the ball in.

As Eddie leapt...

...an elbow went into his side like a dagger.

He crashed to the ground in agony. It had been cleverly done because the linesman saw nothing, not even the assassin's grin. So there was no penalty for the Strikers and the ball was swiftly swept upfield for a raid by the Deaton attack.

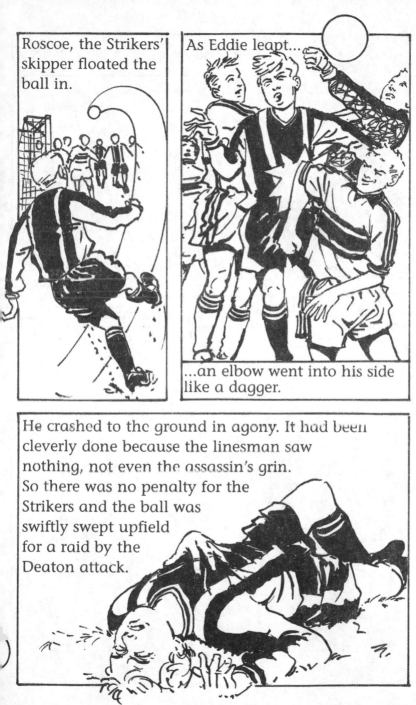

The coach came to help Eddie.

I can hardly breathe. The pain's terrible.

Eddie was as much hurt by that remark as the elbow in his ribs but he said nothing.

Give it a few more minutes. Try to be a bit braver. Don't cry like a baby.

The match restarted but Eddie found it hard to move and when Roscoe hit a long pass to him...

...he saw it coming but couldn't get close to the ball.

Moments later the ref took his arm and pointed to the touchline.

Eddie saw his number eight was being held up. He was to be substituted.

I didn't need to come off, Coach, I'll be fine soon.

Mr Bolton took off his glasses and held them over his large stomach. It was a pose he took when he was angry.

Just because you've got one goal you can't give up and think you've done enough.

You give up all too easily, Eddie, and make out you've got an injury of some sort.

Well that's not good enough for me. I want players on the pitch who work hard all the game.

Eddie tried to protest but the coach wouldn't listen. Eddie had never felt so low. His career with Saxilby was over. He was sure about that. Jimmy Bolton wasn't the sort of man who changed his mind about anything.

35

Oh no! Not another injury.

Eddie was on his feet, staring at the goalmouth where Elliott lay clutching his arm. The ref held up his arm and signalled.

Now I've lost my goalie and run out of subs to put on.

Eddie chased after him.

I'll go in goal.

I do loads of keeping when I train with my brother. I catch everything!

That wasn't quite true but Eddie was desperate to be given another chance on the pitch. Being in goal would surely prove that he didn't lack courage and that he was ready to help the team in any way.

Elliott couldn't lift his arm even to shoulder level.

You'll have to come off, Elliott.

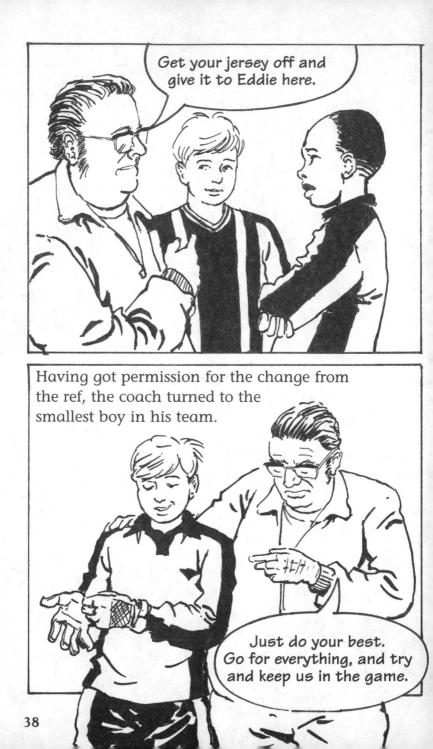

Roscoe patted Eddie on the back as he took up his position between the posts.

Rather you than me!

For some minutes Eddie didn't have anything to do at all as Saxilby's defence kept all raiders at bay. Then Roscoe had the bad luck to give away a corner.

Eddie had to handle the ball for the first time. His nerves were jangling as the ball came over...

...but he timed his jump perfectly.

Got it!

It was in the second half that he faced his greatest test. With Saxilby still leading through Eddie's goal and time running out, Deaton attacked in force. During a goalmouth scramble the ball seemed to hang in the air for a moment.

Eddie hurled himself full-length to grab it – and knocked over Deaton's top striker. Penalty! There could be no argument about it.

Penalty, Ref!

Chapter Four

As the ref took charge, Danny Vengen raced over to Eddie.

Don't worry, you'll save it, Jason always takes their penalties and he hits the ball to the goalie's left.

I used to play in his team at school so I know. Go for it, Eddie!

Eddie nodded his thanks and bounced up and down on his line, hoping to put the kicker off. Would Jason really follow his usual pattern?

He did – and Eddie flung himself leftwards to seize the ball in mid-air.

Jason turned away, head in his hands, and Eddie's team-mates rushed to congratulate him. But the ref was not happy.

Nothing anyone said could change the ref's mind. So Eddie had to face another shot. Would the Deaton player take the same aim or would he try something different? Eddie wished he could read his opponent's mind. But all he could do was remain still and watch Jason's run-up as closely as possible.

He sensed Jason was much more nervous than himself.

Desperate to score, Jason mis-kicked so badly...

...that the ball just trickled towards Eddie who gratefully scooped it up.

Eddie punted the ball away to start another Saxilby attack. No one said a word to Jason and his misery was doubled two minutes later when Danny scored a second goal for Saxilby to take them to an easy win.

Eddie walked off the pitch with Danny, thanking him for his advice about the penalty. Danny shrugged it off.

You saved it, not me. I mean, he might have kicked it the other way or hit a screamer over your head.

It must be a record for a striker to score the first goal and then save a penalty twice over.

The coach should give you a medal, Eddie.

In fact, for once Jimmy Bolton seemed pleased.

You did well there.

How're your ribs now?

Oh, fine.

Eddie replied without thinking. There was some pain but he didn't mention it.

The coach nodded.

Well, after this I might keep you in goal.

But I'm a goal-getter, Coach, not a keeper, I like playing up front.

I'll have to think about that. I'm not making promises about anything.

Chapter Five

Two evenings later Matthew was leaving the house when his mum stopped him.

On your own?

I might meet up with some mates later.

Take Eddie with you and take this to help enjoy yourselves. I'm sick of you two moping around because your football's gone wrong.

Go and forget that game. I'll be glad of some peace to choose my own TV programmes!

Thanks, Mum! Hey Eddie, let's go!

SuperFair came to town in the same week of every year and was the biggest event in the calendar. It was huge and had every kind of ride. All you needed to enjoy it was money.

They parked their bikes and began their spending s████ on the Big Screamer, billed as 'The Most T████ying Ride in the World'.
It didn't terrify them.

Even so, they came off a bit shaken, knees a bit wobbly. But they wouldn't admit that to anyone else.

Come on, let's go on the dodgems.

I bet you can't catch me.

Rubbish! I'll push you all the way round. But when I pass you, you'll never see me again.

Afterwards, they couldn't decide who came off best. Just when each felt he was on top they got tangled up with other cars. They were still arguing about it as they made their way to the Big Dipper. Suddenly a football bounced right in front of them, bringing their argument to a halt. Eddie grabbed the ball.

Where did that come from?

A small boy dashed up holding out his hands.

Thanks for catching it.

The brothers followed the boy to a nearby stall.

The game was simple enough. A long board at ground level contained a row of five holes each a little bigger than a football. A ball was placed on a spot about five metres in front of the board. To win, the kicker had to hit the ball through each hole in turn. It looked easy enough but each shot had to be very accurate to score.

Nobody's done it yet, I did three and then I hit the ball too hard. It bounced off the wall and you caught it.

Are you going to have a go?

Might as well.

As they stood in the queue they watched
a stream of misses as some kickers
overshot the board altogether.

Nobody managed more than two successes.
Even the brothers had to admit it was
much harder than it looked.

Right, young fella,
show us how good you are.
You look as if you know how
to kick a ball properly.

He was right. Matthew's first shot passed clean through the hole.

Spectators applauded.

The second also went in after just clipping the upper edge.

But Matthew didn't let his failure put him off. His final two shots flashed through the holes.

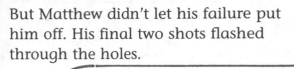

Best of the night, that is. Sorry I can't give you the big prize but you win this top quality football shirt.

Now, let's see what the little'un can do. Can you hit the first five-out-of-five of the night? Go on, son, show us how!

Eddie didn't like being called little'un but it merely fired him up to beat Matthew's score, win his bet and the big prize, whatever it was. The crowd was silent.

He took a couple of steps back and then ran in to hit the ball right-footed.

It went in like a bullet.

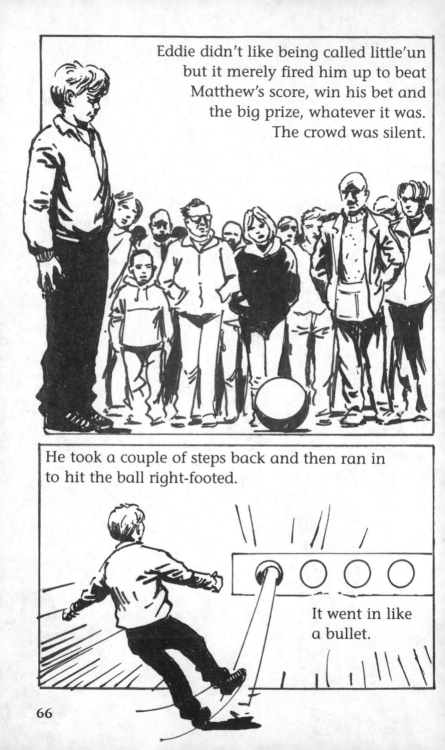

His second shot was just as accurate.

But he feared he'd missed the third. The ball struck the right-hand edge, bounced to the left and then almost in slow motion dropped through the hole. His success was greeted with a real roar this time.

The fourth shot was no trouble at all, going through as cleanly as the first.

As Eddie placed the ball for the vital fifth shot, silence fell like a blanket. No one wanted to upset his concentration. It was clear the crowd wanted him to succeed.

Chapter Six

Eddie took a couple of steps back and focussed on the ball. Suddenly he became aware that people were turning and pointing at something.

The child needed help quickly. He'd wriggled out of his safety belt and fallen on to the track.

People on the Screamer
were telling the little boy
on the track to hold on.
Someone was coming to
help. Eddie couldn't
see the child but in a
few minutes he'd reach
the track. He didn't give
a thought to his own
safety, he just wanted
to help the boy.

Then he heard the wail of the sirens, so he paused.

Just wait there. The fire brigade are here. The child's okay, he's calm.

Eddie halted. There was no point in going on when professional help had arrived. At least the child had known someone was going to save him.

In no time the firemen had their ladders and hoist in place. While some went to rescue the child others helped Eddie from the ironwork and bought him back to the ground.

People ran up to shake his hand.

You were great, Eddie, That took a lot of nerve.

I'm more nervous about this last kick. But I'm going to get that goal and beat your total.

Eddie took a deep breath and fired the ball at the target.

It went through the hole without touching the sides. Even Eddie was surprised. He hadn't been sure he'd do it even though he'd said so. After all, he hadn't had much success lately. Until tonight.

The stall-holder brought out a football and handed it over with a handshake.

It's been signed by top players. You deserve it. You've shown real courage and skill tonight. D'you play in any league team?

Sometimes.

You're on. Can't wait to see you in action. You've pinched my best prize tonight but I'll forgive you when you score the goals that win us the League.